MAPP AT FIFTY

Mapp at Fifty – A story of Mapp & Lucia
in the Style of the Originals by E.F.Benson
Hugh Ashton

ISBN-13: 978-1-912605-66-8

ISBN-10: 1-91-260566-X

Published by j-views Publishing, 2020

www.HughAshtonBooks.com

www.j-views.biz

publish@j-views.biz

j-views Publishing, 26 Lombard Street, Lichfield, WS13 6DR, UK

CONTENTS

INTRODUCTION

I first came into contact with the inhabitants of Tilling at university, and I am afraid at that time much of Benson's subtlety and wit went over my head.

However, Mapp and Lucia have been a constant part of my life ever since I rediscovered them a few years after leaving college, and they formed my specialist subject for *Mastermind* (2019/20 season).

I confess to never having seen the BBC series, but I discovered the McEwan/Scales/Hawthorne DVDs in a shop in a visit to Rye in 2010 or so. I had no idea that they had been on TV, since I had been living in Japan for over twenty years at that time I discovered them. Despite their occasional departure from the script, I still find them to have captured the spirit of Tilling.

Here I have attempted to do the same, with the characters, who, although I thought they were well-known to me, continue to surprise me with their thoughts and speech and actions. Not just the major characters of Mapp, Lucia and Georgie, but all of the Tilling "gentry", who end up being so much more than caricatures of themselves.

Benson's narrative style is hard to imitate, even though putting words into the characters' mouths is relatively easy. Since the words of so many Tillingites fail to express their actual thoughts, Benson often has to insert a little narrative barb to provide his readers with some guidance, lest they naïvely take the speaker at his or her (most often her) word.

Little paradoxes and ironies abound, such as Elizabeth Mapp's use of a handkerchief to conceal the fact that her eyes are not, in fact, filled with tears. Benson's use of these is much more subtle than that of Oscar Wilde, for example, whose wit (as he himself acknowledged) often simply consisted of reversing a popular phrase or saying. In the Riseholme and Tilling books, these reversals and paradoxes are much more closely tied to the characters who speak them, and are used, not so much to demonstrate the cleverness of the author, as to bring the idiosyncrasies of the character into sharper relief. For this reason, these little barbs must be more than mere verbal tricks.

Special thanks are due to the Mapp and Lucia group on Facebook who have encouraged me to hope that this little offering will not be completely unpleasing to you. I am hoping that it will not be my last such visit to Tilling, as there is so much more to write about. So, dear ones, I will not bid you farewell at this time, but *Au reservoir.*

Hugh Ashton, Lichfield, 2020

MAPP AT FIFTY

A STORY OF MAPP & LUCIA
IN THE STYLE OF THE
ORIGINALS BY E.F.BENSON

HUGH ASHTON

J-VIEWS PUBLISHING, LICHFIELD, UK

ONE

"Time, like an ever-rolling stream, bears all its sons away". Elizabeth Mapp-Flint, as she sang these words as part of the choir of the Sunday morning service at Tilling church, reflected to herself that Time also bore away its daughters. Her current thoughts were chiefly concerned with one such daughter, namely herself.

For, although she had long since – indeed, for nearly half a century – known of its approach, the imminent arrival of her fiftieth birthday was preying on her mind. A number of related matters presented themselves to her for her attention, and as she automatically sang the words of the hymn and sat for the sermon, she mulled them over to herself.

Firstly, there was the problem of her age. Without having committed herself outright, she had, ever so delicately, put it about that she had been born several years after the date on her birth certificate. If she wanted to commemorate the half-century of the world's being favoured by the presence of Mrs Elizabeth Mapp-Flint, or Miss Elizabeth Mapp, as she had been styled until only a few years previously, those missing years would have to be explained away. At present, she was unsure how this might be managed, but there was no doubt in her mind that managed it would be.

Next, there was a glorious vision of a chance to outshine Lucia on the occasion of the celebration she was envisaging. Lucia, she remembered, had placed fifty-one candles on the cake that was presented to the guests to mark her fiftieth birthday. Very well, Elizabeth would have fifty-two. There would be no question of Elizabeth providing the quantities of wine that Lucia had served to her guests on that day, but the money saved by the production of the famous ancestral and economical "cup" (a bottle of white wine and quantities of ginger and soda water) would come in handy for the purchase of several hen lobsters, to be used in the production of lobster *à la Riseholme*. The expression on Lucia and Georgie Pillson's faces when they tasted the dish would more than compensate for the extravagance.

Lastly, but by no means least in her thoughts, she had a specific reason in mind for making it known that she had now reached the state of riper years. A few years ago, Lucia had been created Mayor of Tilling, and Elizabeth was of the strong opinion that her (Lucia's) seniority in terms of chronological age had outweighed her (Elizabeth's) seniority as the *doyenne* of Tilling society when it came to selecting the first citizen of Tilling. Through the act of publicly proclaiming her age, Elizabeth was certain that this added dignity would ensure her appointment as the next Mayor, entitled to walk in processions wearing the most fetching robes, preceded by the Town Crier bearing the Municipal Mace, and pointed out and photographed by tourists as the embodiment of English civic tradition.

These matters having been duly dealt with, Elizabeth sank into a pleasurable reverie regarding the birthday gift that she would demand – no, she would not demand, but gently suggest to Benjy that he present to her to mark the start of her sixth decade of life. She was awakened from visions of sable coats (vulgarly opulent, and in any case far beyond the reach of Major Benjy's purse) and a week in Monte Carlo, when she heard the Padre intoning "And now to God the Father, God the Son, and God the Holy Ghost".

With a start she realised that she had not heard a word of what he had been saying for the past (she glanced surreptitiously at her watch) twenty-three minutes, thereby depriving her of the pleasure of criticising the sermon to all and sundry over the course of the coming week.

TWO

A t breakfast the next morning, Elizabeth called her husband's attention to the picture hanging on the wall behind him.

"Much as it reminds me of dear Aunt Caroline," she said with a reflective air, "it does not seem a suitable subject for our dining-room."

Major Benjamin Mapp-Flint turned to view the offending work of art. It was hard to say how his wife could see any resemblance to her aunt, with the painting depicting as it did a near naked Saint Sebastian regarding the arrows that threatened to turn him into a human porcupine with an expression of disdain mixed with boredom.

"Don't see why it reminds you of your aunt,"

he remarked, slicing the top off his boiled egg. "Nothing like the photographs I've seen of her."

"Naughty boy," Elizabeth scolded him playfully. "It was left to me by Aunt Caroline as a family heirloom together with Mallards, where we would still be living, if it weren't for those odious schemes of Lucia's." She forced a pretty little catch into her voice at the mention of Mallards, but Benjy had learned by experience that this was a diversionary path best left untrodden. Instead, he continued to gaze at Sebastian, who stared back unblinkingly.

"Do you know," he said after a while, "I don't remember seeing that picture before."

This was hardly surprising. The painting in question, a nineteenth-century copy of a painting hanging in a dusty corner of the Uffizi and attributed to an anonymous pupil of Andrea del Sarto, had hung in an unused spare bedroom of Mallards, and following the move to Grebe, had stayed in its packing chest until the previous evening, when Elizabeth had removed one of her own watercolour landscapes and hung Sebastian in its place.

"Oh, you men!" she laughed mirthlessly in an ascending minor key. "But I forgive you," she added magnanimously. "It takes a woman's taste to make a home, after all."

"Well, I don't like it there, either," he hastened to assure her. "But what will you put in its place? One of your watercolours would look nice there."

Elizabeth appeared to consider this for a moment, and shook her head. "No, sweet of you, Benjy-boy, to suggest that one of my little efforts would fit the bill, but I think something more striking, and more expressive of the character and personalities of the present occupants of this house, would be suitable. A painting that speaks of the character of the inhabitants."

She watched with interest as he mentally assembled the bricks that she had presented to him into an edifice.

"A portrait, perhaps?" he suggested.

She laughed gaily and dismissively, thereby signifying her approval of the idea.

"And it's your birthday coming up, isn't it, Liz? Say no more." He tapped the side of his nose in what he took to be a significant manner.

Ah, the final keystone of the arch was now in place. Pleased with what had turned out to have been an easy morning's work, she encouraged him to pile his toast extravagantly with butter and marmalade. Indeed, if it had not been for the early hour, she would have poured him a whisky and soda with her own hands.

The truth was that, after dear quaint Irene Coles had painted her portrait of Lucia, which Elizabeth had been instrumental in persuading the Council to reject, Elizabeth had been insanely jealous of the fact that a recognised artist – the creator of the Royal Academy's Picture of the Year, no less, had seen fit to depict Lucia in solitary splendour. It was true that Elizabeth and Benjy formed key elements of Irene's "Birth of Venus", which had been acclaimed by eminent critics on both sides of the Atlantic, but there was a satirical and mocking element about the painting, which had made itself slowly apparent to Elizabeth once the first flush of excitement had worn off.

A portrait by Irene of Elizabeth Mapp-Flint, whether or not it included Benjy-boy, would go a long way towards soothing the feathers that had been ruffled by Irene's paintbrush. Satisfied that matters were proceeding satisfactorily, she countermanded the scrag end of mutton that was to have been their lunch, and replaced it with lamb chump chops.

THREE

Major Benjamin Mapp-Flint was proud of the intuition that had led him to interpret Elizabeth's wishes so accurately. If the truth were to be told, he was somewhat excited at the thought of the portrait. So she wanted a portrait of her husband, did she (for in his mind, it was only right and proper that if there were to be only one portrait, it should be of the man of the house)? Very well, it would be the best possible painting that Major Benjamin Mapp-Flint could procure.

He was due to meet the Padre at ten at the links for their golf, but decided to telephone him instead, pleading a sore throat that he was sure presaged influenza, and postponing their game indefinitely.

Instead, he walked into Tilling with the express purpose of calling on Irene Coles and requesting her services to create his likeness on canvas. Arriving at Irene's house, Taormina, he knocked on the door, only to be hailed from across the street by Irene herself, carrying her marketing basket. "Benjy-wenjy!" she cried out to him in tones that must have carried across the whole of Tilling. "Tell me you have left Mapp, and come to throw in your lot with me, dearest. Oh, do say it is so!"

He was quite at a loss, as so often with Irene, as to how best to reply to her greeting, and for once, she took pity on his obvious embarrassment. "Never mind my nonsense," she told him, not unkindly. "Now do come inside, find yourself a chair without any paint on it, if there is still one left, sit down, and tell me what you have come to see me about. It is me, and not Lucy, that you have come to see, isn't it?" she added, with a flash of that humour that Elizabeth was pleased to call "quaint".

Once he had found his seat, Major Benjy's confidence was restored. "I'd like you to paint a portrait," he began.

"I might be able to manage that," Irene told

him. "I am considered by some to have some talent in that direction. And who, may I ask, is the lucky subject who is to be honoured by sitting for me?"

"Why, it is to be me, of course. It's to be my birthday present to Liz. She'll be fifty years old next week."

Irene, who knew that Lucia had for some time been attempting to establish Elizabeth's true age (as opposed to the officially promulgated value), stored this piece of information away for future use. "And when is this to be done?" she asked.

"I was hoping we could be finished before lunch," he replied.

Irene let out a hoot of laughter. "My dear sweet Major Benjy-wenjy," she shrieked, mopping her eyes with a large spotted handkerchief cheerfully decorated with splashes of green paint. "The preliminary sketches alone would be two or three days of sittings. Then you must give me a week to decide on the treatment of the raw material, and a further month to exercise my brilliance and convert it into a finished painted form."

"I see," he told her in a dejected tone.

"I suppose," Irene went on in a reflective way, "that you couldn't persuade Mapp to delay her birthday for a couple of months? No?" She pulled her pipe from her pocket and filled it, obviously in thought. "And then, of course, there is the question of my fee. It's not that I really care about the money, but one has to live, don't you know? How big is this portrait to be?"

By now, Major Benjy was beginning to wish he had never started this business. "About this big," he told Irene, making gestures with his hands.

"A portrait of that size would cost you seventy-five," Irene told him.

"Pounds?" he exclaimed, horrified. The sum named came to almost all the money in the world that he could still call his and his alone.

"Guineas," she corrected him. "And that's a special Tilling price. If you lived anywhere but Tilling, it would be one hundred and twenty-five."

"Then I think I'd better look somewhere else."

"Good luck finding another genius in this tiny place," Irene told him. "Of course, you could always ask Georgie Pillson. He told me that he'd once given Lucia a portrait as a Christmas present."

"Did he, by Jove?" The idea of asking Georgie for a favour, and the necessity of spending prolonged periods of time sitting for the man he had once unkindly dubbed 'Miss Milliner Michael-Angelo' was not one that appealed to the Major, but needs must, he told himself. And he was sure that Georgie would not ask for anything like seventy-five guineas for his services. "Then I will go and talk to him. Mum's the word, mind, about all this business."

"My lips are sealed," Irene told him as he left, with the full intention of breaking that seal whenever the occasion seemed most appropriate to so do.

FOUR

Much as he disliked the idea of approaching Georgie and requesting his assistance in the matter of the portrait, Major Mapp-Flint felt he was faced with little choice. He could, if he had preferred, have approached Mr. Wyse or Susan Wyse with his request, but having been exposed to samples of their work in the Tilling Art Society's annual exhibitions, he was unwilling for his features to be depicted by either.

Grudgingly, he admitted that Miss Milliner Michael-Angelo's works displayed a degree of skill that was matched only by those of Lucia (always excepting the recognised skills and talent of Irene Coles). And, mere man that he was, he had wit enough to perceive that any work of art by Lucia would be as unwelcome in Grebe as if Lucia herself were to occupy the spare bedroom and preside over the breakfast table.

He was standing outside the door and steeling himself to address the redoubtable Foljambe, Georgie's extremely pretty and devoted parlourmaid, or else Grosvenor, who performed the same services for Lucia as did Foljambe for Georgie, when the door opened, and out stepped Georgie Pillson himself.

"Ha! What a stroke of luck, old man," Major Benjy exclaimed. "I was just about to ring your bell, and... and..."

"Here I am," said Georgie brightly. He was in an excellent mood. The chartreuse cashmere scarf that he had ordered from London had arrived the day before, and it matched his tie and socks beautifully. He was wearing it now as a protection against the morning chills and damp that came from the marshes.

"Quite so," replied the Major. "Er... I was wondering if you would be able to help me. It's a rather delicate matter." He dropped his voice, all too aware of the fact that the garden-room of Mallards overlooked him and Georgie, and it was possible, nay, probable, that Lucia was in that room and was aware of his presence. "No offence to your good wife, but I would sooner she didn't hear what I am about to say. May we walk together to the town?"

"Certainly," Georgie told him, by now intrigued by the air of secrecy with which the Major had invested his mission, whatever it might prove to be.

"As I say, this is rather delicate, and I hope it won't sound too presumptuous," began Major Benjy as the oddly-assorted couple made their way to the High Street. "Liz has set her heart on having my portrait painted. It's for her fiftieth birthday, you know."

"I know," said Georgie, who was hearing the news about Elizabeth's age for the first time. "I mean, I know about her birthday, not about the portrait."

"Well, the thing about a portrait is," the Major went on, "that someone has to paint it, if you see what I mean."

"Yes?" Georgie put an encouraging note into his voice.

"And it has to be someone in Tilling, you see, because if I went away somewhere else to get it done, Liz would get suspicious."

"I see," said Georgie. "Well, there's always Irene Coles."

"Ah, you've hit the nail square on the head, old man. I went to see her about it, and she said it would take a long time. At least a month, and Liz has her birthday next week." Major Benjy did not consider it worth mentioning the amount of money involved at this stage.

"I see," said Georgie again. "Tarsome."

"So I was wondering if you..." He left Georgie to fill in the remainder of the sentence.

"...if I might be able to paint your portrait?"

"That's the ticket."

Georgie appeared to be thinking hard. "I'm not very good at portraits," he admitted at last.

"Nonsense. I've seen your pictures in our little exhibitions, and if I'm to be honest with you," the Major told Georgie, lying like Ananias, "your little masterpieces are the stars of the show."

"Well, if you say so." Georgie was most heartened by this praise from an unexpected quarter. He was seized with a sudden inspiration. Given his usual subjects for portraits – old ladies, and boys holding cricket bats – it seemed to him that the subject and pose for Major Benjy's portrait were ready and waiting for his brush. "I could paint you at the links," he suggested, "holding a golf-club."

"That sounds like just the thing. Since I go

to the links anyway, then Liz will be none the wiser about our little secret, will she? Ha-ha. Maybe we can start this afternoon?"

Georgie felt he was being carried along by some unstoppable Juggernaut, but recovered himself enough to make a timid mention of the fee for his services.

"I mean to say," he told the Major, "there's the cost of the paint and the canvas, not to mention my time. What it comes down to is that I couldn't possibly consider doing it for under eight pounds."

"Make them guineas," the Major told him expansively, heaving a large mental sigh of relief. Naturally, he would not be expected to pay Georgie's tram or taxi fare to and from the links, but a sum of eight guineas seemed much more reasonable to him than quaint Irene's seventy-five.

"Most generous of you," Georgie answered, inwardly berating himself for not having demanded a higher fee.

"So we'll say two o'clock at the golf clubhouse, then?" suggested the Major.

"Very well," answered Georgie. "*Au reservoir,*" and went on to finish his marketing before hurrying back to tell Lucia the news.

FIVE

Mrs Emmeline Pillson, Georgie's wife of several years, and formerly the wife of the now deceased Philip Lucas, and by a process of Italianisation "*la Lucia*", or simply "Lucia" as she was now known to all, had indeed seen her husband in conversation with Major Benjamin Mapp-Flint, and was puzzled (an unusual circumstance for her) by the possible topic of their conversation.

When he returned from his marketing, Lucia waited for him to broach the subject. The crude method of asking him directly was not Lucia's way - it was left to lesser souls to adopt such an approach.

"Guess," he told her, in the best manner of

Riseholme, the Elizabethan village where they had both resided before her conquest of Tilling society.

Lucia had a fair idea of some of the conversation, but decided to tease Georgie a little. "He wants to teach you to play golf?"

"No. It concerns Elizabeth."

"Her birthday?"

"Tarsome of you. How did you guess that?" Georgie was a little put out by Lucia's question.

"I have my little ways."

"Oh, do stop teasing, and tell me," Georgie implored her. "Don't be so *cattiva* and *misteriosa*."

"When Elizabeth was my Mayoress, and later one of my Councillors, all of her details were written in the civic records in the Town Hall."

"So you know how old she will be as well? Major Benjy let that slip without realising."

"Fifty," Lucia answered him simply.

Rather than being downcast at Lucia's appropriation of his news, Georgie found a bright side to the matter. "And the joy of it is that we know, and she doesn't know that we know. Should we tell Diva and Evie and the Padre?"

"No, let us keep it a secret. We should let them have the joy of discovering these things by themselves." Georgie did not believe her for a second. Lucia hoarded such secrets, and released them to the world on occasions when they would have the most effect. "But surely that was not all that you and he were discussing?" The direct approach now seemed a little more likely to produce results, and though she would never admit it to anyone, least of all to Georgie, she burned to know the subject that had been under discussion. "Was he asking you for advice on the present he will give her?"

Georgie nodded but remained silent.

"What did you tell him? Let me think." Her brow furrowed in thought for a minute, and she shrugged. "A set of golf clubs?"

"Oo is not getting vewy warm," Georgie told her, using the baby-talk that they used together in private.

"No," she admitted after a pause. "I confess I cannot guess. Too diffy."

"He wants to give her a portrait."

"A portrait of Elizabeth? And you to paint it?"

Georgie shook his head. "No, he wants to give her a portrait of himself, and he wants me to paint it." The words came tumbling out in a rush.

"Well! Of all the self-centred... Did Elizabeth ask for a portrait of him?"

"He never told me that she did."

"Then I think we may assume that she did

not," Lucia said firmly. "Let me guess. I believe that she mentioned a portrait, with Elizabeth being who she is, intending that it should be a portrait of her, and Benjy, being who he is, believed that she wanted a portrait of him."

"It would be just like her," Georgie agreed. "Not telling him directly, but hinting at it in that way of hers. And just like him to get it wrong. Oh, I do hope we are invited to the party. I want to see her face when she sees the portrait."

"But why has he asked you of all people to paint it?"

"I'm sure I don't know," he replied, somewhat nettled.

Lucia was quick to extricate herself from the quicksand into which she appeared to have stumbled. "I meant no insult to your artistic skills, my dear. Only that, with a Royal Academician in the town, quaint Irene would seem to be his first port of call."

"Of course it was. He told me that she told him that it would take a month for the portrait to be finished, and so it would not be ready for Elizabeth's birthday."

Lucia laughed her silvery laugh. "But you and I know that is nonsense, do we not? Why, we have seen her start and complete a painting in the course of a single day." She paused for a moment. "I trust Benjy is paying you for this work?"

"Yes, and if you ask me how much, I shall tell you that it is none of your business. It is a matter between me and him."

"As you wish. But I am willing to believe that when he asked Irene – if indeed he did, which is by no means certain – that she presented him with a price that he was unwilling to pay. Whatever he is paying you, Georgino *mio*, is *troppo poco*. Too little."

"In any case, I start at two o'clock. I am meeting him at the golf clubhouse."

"May I come along?"

"Most definitely not." Georgie was firm. "It will upset me, and it will also upset my subject."

"Oo poor boy," said Lucia. "*Troppo sensitivo*." She was not sure if that last word was Italian or not, but Georgie let it pass. "*Un po' de Mozartino* to settle your nerves?"

Without waiting for a reply, she led the way to the piano stool, and seated herself at the treble end.

"Dwefful diffy for poor ickle me," she said. "But lovely bass part for oo. Ready? *Uno, duo, tre...*"

SIX

After this musical interlude, luncheon was eaten in near-silence and in Georgie's case, with an air of anxious anticipation. There was only one topic of conversation worth pursuing, and Lucia knew better than to quiz Georgie too hard on it.

He hurriedly collected his sketchpad and all his painting equipment and prepared to depart.

"Should I take a taxi or the steam-tram?" he asked anxiously.

"A taxi, of course," Lucia told him firmly. "I am sure Major Benjy will offer to pay for it. And if he doesn't offer, then you must drop heavy hints on the subject."

"Very well, then," said Georgie. "I'll ask Foljambe to use the telephone to order one."

Lucia laughed. "I have anticipated you, Georgino *mio*," she informed him. "I have already asked Cadman to take you to the links. Cadman can wait for you, and bring you back. And Major Benjy too, if he wishes."

"Well, you are kind," Georgie said admiringly. "And kind to Major Benjy, too."

"Always a pleasure to help one's friends," Lucia replied.

She watched Georgie advise Cadman on the safe stowage of his sketching and painting materials before settling himself into the back seat of the Royce and being driven off in the direction of the links.

With a smile, Lucia started to busy herself in the garden-room with the arrangement of some flowers which she had picked that morning, when Grosvenor entered to tell her that Irene Coles had called.

"Show her in," Lucia told her, and was just placing the last flower in the vase when Irene appeared in the doorway, dressed in her usual costume of a paint-spattered man's shirt and corduroy trousers. Much to Lucia's relief, she was not smoking her clay pipe.

"My angel!" Irene exclaimed. Since Lucia had

arrived in Tilling, Irene had been her most staunch admirer and supporter, developing an affection for her which was almost embarrassing at times. "Those hollyhocks! Too vibrant! Too colourful! They kill the room."

"And what would you suggest, Irene?"

"Nettles. Don't you know, I am in love with nettles. I have been since yesterday. They appear so harmless, and yet you only have to brush against them and... When I die, I want to be reincarnated as a nettle."

"Irene, you're talking rubbish," said Lucia firmly.

"I know I am, and you're so sweet to listen to it. But let me tell you my news."

"Major Benjy?"

Irene's face fell, but only a little. "Did Georgie tell you?"

"A little, but you may give me the details."

"Well," said Irene, settling herself down in an armchair, "Major Benjy came to see me."

"Georgie told me," Lucia answered her. "About a portrait?"

"Yes, that was it. It seems that Mapp had been dropping hints about how she wanted her picture painted, and Major Benjy, God save the King and *quai hai* and all that, bless him, thought she wanted a picture of him. So he came to see me."

"And?" Lucia leaned forward, eager to hear the conversation at first hand.

"I told him that it would take a month or more. Was that very wrong of me?"

Lucia smiled. "I don't think so. How long would it have taken you?"

"A morning. And perhaps half of an afternoon. And then I think he expected me to paint him for free. So I soon put that right."

"May I be permitted to ask how much you suggested to him?"

"Of course you may. I was just about to tell you, anyway. Seventy-five."

"Seventy-five pounds? Dear me, that is a lot of money."

"Seventy-five guineas," Irene corrected her. "We artists move in a world of guineas, not mere pounds. He seemed somewhat surprised and rushed off to see Georgie as soon as I suggested it."

"You suggested it?" asked Lucia, somewhat surprised.

"Of course. He's quite my favourite person in Tilling – after you, of course," Irene added hurriedly. "Do you know, if he wasn't already married to you, and if he wasn't quite so much of an old maid, I would be very tempted to take him under my wing and tuck him up in bed every night. He is a dear, isn't he?" She broke off. "I suppose I shouldn't be talking like this about your husband, should I? Never mind, he's safe with you. I won't steal him away from you."

"What nonsense you do talk," Lucia smiled indulgently.

"Now it's your turn to tell me," Irene said. "How much will Georgie's little painting cost Major Benjy?"

"That's a secret between him and me," smiled Lucia. Of course, it was a secret between Georgie and himself, but Lucia had no intention of saying that to Irene.

"Oh, you are a tease," said Irene. "Can I have a cocktail?"

Lucia rang the bell for Grosvenor, and requested a cocktail for Irene, and a lemonade for herself.

"I know we're both very fond of Georgie, but tell me, angel, can he really paint portraits? I've seen his pretty little watercolours of Tilling, and just the thing they are for tourists to buy and gather dust on their walls when they get home. But portraits, dear one?"

For answer, Lucia merely pointed to the picture of herself which Georgie had painted at Riseholme on the orders of Olga Bracely (though Lucia was unaware of the circumstances surrounding the commissioning of the work). Irene got up from her chair and squinted at it.

"Well, it is you," she said. "But it lacks soul. Not that that would be a problem with Major Benjy, of course, since there is no soul to depict."

"Naughty girl," Lucia replied. "Naughty to say that about poor Major Benjy."

"Well, it's true, isn't it? And if you and everyone else don't say it out loud, I'm sure you think it."

Grosvenor appeared with the drinks, and Irene took her glass before continuing. "If Georgie finds himself in difficulties, tell him that my door is always open to him." She drank off her cocktail in one gulp and set down the glass. "Now I must be going. The clouds over the marsh as I was coming here put me in mind of Armageddon, and I have to capture the colours before the light fades."

"*Au reservoir*," Lucia called after her retreating figure.

SEVEN

Lucia was resting her eyes while relaxing on the sofa, when she heard the sound of her car drawing up outside Mallards.

"Goodness me!" she said, rubbing her eyes as she glanced at the clock. "I had no idea it was nearly five o'clock." She arose hastily, and seated herself at the desk, snatching up a pen. It would never do for her to be discovered having newly awakened from a nap, or worse yet, napping.

A moment later, Georgie came in and flung himself with a deep sigh full length on the sofa recently vacated by Lucia.

"Poor ickle Georgino," said Lucia, not unsympathetically. "Was it really so dwefful?"

"Tarsome rather than dreadful," said Georgie. "He would keep on talking so much and moving around. I could hardly draw a line, he was bothering me so much."

"What was he talking about?" Lucia asked avidly. Major Benjy's unguarded conversations often led to revelations about Elizabeth Mapp-Flint and her world which, when disseminated, enlivened the life of Tilling.

"Oh, nothing, really. He would keep going on about India and the tigers he'd shot." Georgie drew a tactful veil over the Major's recounted amorous exploits. The memory of his mention of the "Pride of Poona" at a dinner party given by Mr Wyse still had the power to stir dormant tongues. "Oh, there is one thing he let slip. Guess."

"Elizabeth is learning to drive a motor-car?"

"No. It's to do with the birthday party. A surprise guest."

"The Prince of Wales? The Lord Mayor of London?" Lucia's powers of sarcasm were considerable, but hardly ever deployed against Georgie, and he resented it.

"No, no," he told her with a touch of annoyance in his voice. "It's her sister. Elizabeth's sister, Catherine."

"Have we ever heard of her before? We have

not, have we? Older or younger? Why haven't we seen her before? Did Major Benjy tell you that?"

"So many questions. Thereby hangs a tale," Georgie told her. "Let's have tea, and I'll tell you all about it."

When tea had been served and Georgie and Lucia were occupied with teacups and scones, he resumed his narrative.

"All that I know is what I was told this afternoon. Major Benjy may be mistaken in what he told me, and I may not be reporting his words accurately."

"I am sure you have remembered everything perfectly," Lucia assured him.

"Well," said Georgie, taking a sip of his tea, "Catherine is apparently Elizabeth's older sister—"

"How old?" Lucia asked excitedly.

"Major Benjy didn't know when I asked him," Georgie said. "But she has a son, Harold, who is just starting a new job in the City, apparently."

"And her husband? There is a husband, is there not?"

"There was a husband," Georgie corrected her. "He died of the influenza after the War."

"A nephew?" Lucia mused reflectively. "I seem to remember Diva telling me something about him in connection with the day that the Prince of Wales apparently came to Tilling. Before our time here, so it's only hearsay, and we may therefore discount it, I feel."

Georgie, who was well aware that Lucia was capable of erecting and subsequently moving mountains of news which she created from a molehill of hearsay, held his peace.

"So just the sister is coming? Not the nephew?"

"Just the sister," Georgie assured her. "But I haven't told you the best bit yet. According to Major Benjy, when Elizabeth and Catherine were younger, they used to come and stay with Aunt Caroline at Mallards..."

"And probably played that remarkable old corpse of a Blumenfelt piano," Lucia laughed.

"Quite possibly," agreed Georgie. "Anyway, Catherine was the aunt's favourite, and she was assured by the aunt that when she – I mean the aunt – died, Catherine was to be left Mallards, and Elizabeth was to inherit a small sum of money."

"But Elizabeth inherited Mallards," Lucia pointed out. "At least, that is what she has always told us."

"So she did. When the sisters were a little older, Aunt Caroline disinherited Catherine other than for a few little knick-knacks of no particular value, and Elizabeth received the house and the money."

"Why?"

"According to Major Benjy, Catherine was a leader of the Suffragette movement, campaigning for Votes for Women before the War, and Aunt Caroline thoroughly disapproved of the notion that women should have the vote."

"How thrilling!" exclaimed Lucia, her eyes shining. "Did Catherine chain herself to railings or anything of that nature? One must disapprove of actions which are against the law of the land, but at the same time, one cannot help but feel admiration for those who are prepared to suffer for their deeply held principles."

"I am afraid I don't know the answer to that."

"Perhaps we could find out. If she was taking part in these Suffragette outrages before she was married, she would be named Catherine Mapp, would she not? I am sure there must be accounts of her doings somewhere. What it must feel like to be a campaigner for democracy such as that!"

"Well, women have the vote now," Georgie pointed out, "so there is no sense in your trying to copy her."

Lucia fixed him with a gimlet-like eye.

"Georgie, *carissimo*," she said firmly. "I hope you do not imagine that I would try to emulate such actions and outrages as those carried out by the Suffragettes."

"Of course not," said Georgie, though in fact he had been thinking precisely that. Lucia, as he knew from experience, was perfectly capable of seizing the ideas and enthusiasms of another and passing them off as her own 'stunts'.

As if she had been reading his thoughts, Lucia swiftly changed the subject away from the Suffragettes.

"We must make her welcome when she arrives, Georgie. Tea, do you think, or dinner?"

"If you must," said Georgie, "though I don't imagine she will relish the idea of visiting a house which was once promised to her, and which she failed to inherit. But if you really must, then tea. If you invited her to dinner, then you would have to invite the Mapp-Flints as well, and that would be too sickening for words. Imagine Elizabeth crowing over both her and you at the same time."

Lucia shuddered. "How right you are, Georgie, to consider these things. Yes, I see what you mean. Tea, then, by all means, but at Diva's as my guest. If I give Diva my recipe for *éclairs*, do you think she might be persuaded to serve them to us?"

"You can try," said Georgie, doubtfully. "I think Diva is happier with the recipes she knows. But yes, you are perfectly right to think of Diva's as a solution. No man's land, as it were."

"And now," Lucia said, "for the whole point of the exercise, that is to say, your portrait of Major Benjy. May ickle me have *un piccolo sguardo*?"

"If you mean a little look, the answer is 'no'," Georgie told her firmly. "It needs a lot more work, though no more sittings, thank goodness. I have the lines all worked out, and it will only take me a few more days before it is finished."

"I should mention that Irene called and asked me to tell you that her door is always open to you should you ever feel that you need any assistance with the picture. And, of course, I might also be able to put a few little hints and tips your way."

"Well, that is kind of her," said Georgie. "And of you, of course. But I will wait until I am stuck in a rut before asking anyone for their help."

"May I ask how you are portraying Major Benjy?" asked Lucia.

"You remember those pictures I painted in

Riseholme of the boys playing cricket? I used the same pose for the Major, but I substituted a golf club for the cricket bat. I think he was quite taken with the idea. But then I asked him to smile, and that was quite enough for me. He'd come up with a story from his Indian days and then smile, and then another story and then smile. I shall dream of hyænas and elephants and tigers all night, I know I shall."

"Hyænas don't live in India," Lucia corrected him.

"I know they don't, but they make this terrible laughing sound, I believe, and so does Major Benjy. I can hear it now."

"You poor lamb. We shall have a nice quiet evening at home," she consoled him.

EIGHT

The next day, Lucia went to do her market-ing, and almost collided with Diva Plaistow, who appeared to be deep in thought.

"Sorry. Busy thinking," Diva told her. "Cocoa or coffee?"

"To drink? Coffee, definitely."

"No. Icing for shortbread fingers."

"I've never heard of anyone putting icing on shortbread," Lucia told her.

"Nor me." Diva said, "Thought it was time someone tried it."

"Chocolate, then," said Lucia.

"Glad you think so. My thought too. Any news?"

Lucia hesitated, but only for a second.

"Elizabeth's birthday party. Guess who's coming?"

"I can tell you one person who's not been invited? Have you?"

"No, nor I. I'm sure the invitations are on their way, though."

"Who's coming to the party, then?"

"Elizabeth's sister, the famous Suffragette."

Diva's round face grew even rounder as her jaw dropped, and her mouth opened in surprise.

"Elizabeth has a famous sister? She's never said anything about her to us. How did you find out?"

"A little birdie told me. What a treat for us all to meet her, and how deliciously modest of Elizabeth not to mention her famous sister."

"Ho!" said Diva.

"What do you mean by 'Ho'?" Lucia asked her, apparently a little put out by Diva's reaction.

"I'm sure you're telling me exactly what your little birdie told you, Lucia, but I don't believe your little birdie got the right end of the stick."

"We shall see," said Lucia frostily, and entered Twistevant's to order some Smyrna figs.

"Padre!" Diva called to the Reverend Bartlett, who happened to be in a somewhat Scotch mood that morning, with a Chaucerian turn of phrase overlaying the Northern British with which his speech had become inextricably flavoured.

"Good morrow to ye, Mistress Plaistow," he greeted her. "And prithee, is there nae news to be had this fair morn?"

"Elizabeth. Sister. Birthday party," Diva told him.

"Hoots, I never heard tell of any sister to her. There's nae such body, I'll warrant ye that."

"She did mention her nephew once," Diva reminded him.

"Och, that was just a wee story to cover her bitty confusion that day the Prince of Wales came and the puir lassie dropped her flag when she fell over in the road trying to make her curtsey to him."

"Now, that's most unfair, Kenneth," squeaked his wife, Evie, who had crept up, mouse-like and unobserved, behind them, and been listening to the conversation. "Why shouldn't Elizabeth Mapp-Flint have a sister if she wants?"

"Nae reason whatsoever," her husband replied, unabashed, "but I'll believe in her when I see her."

"Anyway, tell us all about the party," Evie implored Diva. "Kenneth and I haven't heard anything."

"Nor I," said Diva, "Lucia told me just now that there was to be a party, and that the sister was coming."

"Oh, Lucia told you? Who told her, I wonder?" asked Evie.

"Some little birdie," Diva told her. "That's all she told me."

NINE

When Lucia returned home after this interlude, she discovered Georgie in the
garden-room in a state of great excitement.

"Here she is!" he exclaimed, pointing to various volumes that were spread out all over the
table.

"Elizabeth's sister?" asked Lucia, her mind
still running on the conversation she'd had
with Diva.

"Yes. Look here." Georgie pointed to a page
of *Who's Who*.

Lucia picked up the volume and read out,
"'Catherine Sedgewick (*née* Mapp)'. That
sounds like her, does it not, Georgie? 'Born...
Elder sister of Elizabeth... Married...' Oh, he

died just after the War, as you told me, Georgie. Influenza, no doubt... Oh—!" Lucia suddenly broke off.

"What is it?" Georgie enquired.

"She's a Member of Parliament!" exclaimed Lucia. "It's extraordinary that Elizabeth hasn't made something of her famous sister."

"I agree. Even if she has been a Suffragette, you would have thought that Elizabeth would have mentioned her before," Georgie reflected. "But you should read on, though," he commanded Lucia.

"Socialist!" Lucia read in a tone of disbelief. "A Member of Parliament for some town up in the North. Well, I never! I am not surprised after all that Elizabeth has kept her hidden. A Socialist, and a Suffragette! Hardly in the same class as Mr Garroby-Ashton – you remember him, Georgie, our Member at Riseholme. A most distinguished man, and his wife was delightful. I recall – oh, how I remember – taking tea with the Garroby-Ashtons on the Terrace of the House of Commons, and the dear Prime Minister inviting Pepino and me for a little informal visit to Chequers." She sighed as if lost in the past.

"But look a little further," Georgie urged her.

"She has— oh no, Georgie! She was awarded

the Member of the British Empire two years ago."

"Just like Susan Wyse."

Lucia seemed to be deep in thought. "I didn't realise they gave these things to Socialists, though, or if they did, that Socialists accepted them."

"It's going to be interesting to see what happens when she arrives at the party wearing her MBE," said Georgie. "Susan Wyse has taken to wearing hers at every tea-party or dinner where she has been invited, or where she is the hostess. She even came into Diva's for tea the other day with it pinned to her dress."

"No!" exclaimed Lucia.

"She told us that her maid had forgotten to remove it from the dress that she'd been wearing the day before. Of course, we all pretended to believe her."

"Poor Susan," said Lucia with a pitying look. "With her sables and her Royce and her Order, she never seems to be content. Always seeking to outdo others, and make herself the most important person in the group."

Though Georgie was perfectly capable of replying to this, he felt that his answer would not be appreciated by Lucia, and he changed the subject.

"Will we go to the party, then?"

"If Elizabeth deigns to send us an invitation, certainly."

"Oh, I quite forgot," said Georgie with a start. "The excitement of discovering Elizabeth's sister put it completely out of my mind." He held up an envelope and drew out a card. "Withers dropped it in when she came to do the marketing."

"Let me see," said Lucia, almost snatching it from Georgie's fingers. "Here we are. 'Major and Mrs Mapp-Flint request the pleasure of the company of Mr and Mrs Pillson at a *soirée* to be held at 7:30 pm on Thursday next at Grebe. Black tie.'" Lucia spoke in a scornful tone. "'*Soirée*' indeed! I am sure she will try to keep the wine out of poor Major Benjy's sight."

"'*Soirée*', though," mused Georgie. "What sort of entertainment do you think she will provide?"

"A speech by the Honourable Member for Keythorpe?" suggested Lucia. "Or perhaps a few rousing choruses of the Suffragettes to remind us of that dear time, so long ago, when Elizabeth was young?"

Sarcasm was not Lucia's usual weapon of choice, and Georgie felt that matters were getting out of hand. In any event, he felt somewhat aggrieved that Lucia had not recognised his cleverness in finding out the details of Elizabeth's sister.

"I'm sure I don't know," he said. "Whatever happens, it is sure to be interesting."

Lucia caught the note of resentment in his voice, and swiftly moved to restore harmony. "How skilful of you to find out about Elizabeth's sister," she told him. "How did you manage it?"

"I remembered that I have a book on the Suffragettes that Olga Bracely lent to me once and I never returned to her. I found Catherine Mapp's name there, and it also mentioned that she had later married a man named William Sedgewick. Since she had been quite famous before the War, I thought it might be possible to find her in this year's *Who's Who*, and so it proved to be."

"Well, that really was clever of you," said Lucia. "And so quickly, too."

"So do we tell everyone?" asked Georgie.

Lucia appeared to consider the idea for a moment. "No, I think not," she answered at length. "Just think what fun it will be if we don't tell anyone. Much as I appreciate Mr Wyse's exquisite taste and sense of good manners, imagine how a Socialist will react when he starts talking about the Contessa."

"Or Susan about her MBE, when Catherine Sedgewick also has been presented with the same award."

"Oh, I do hope decorations will be worn," said Lucia. "We can't miss this party for the world."

"I can't help feeling a little sorry for Elizabeth, though," said Georgie. "What a horrid birthday it might turn out to be for her. A picture of Major Benjy, instead of her portrait—"

"—but painted most beautifully by you, Georgie," put in Lucia.

"Yes, well, we will see about that, won't we? The point is, it doesn't matter who painted it, because the subject of the picture isn't what she is expecting, I am sure. And then her sister. I don't see how she is going to mix in Tilling society."

"She may find something in common with Irene's quaint notions," Lucia pointed out. "I'm sure she is a perfectly decent sort of person, once you take out the Socialism and the Suffragettes."

"And the fact that she is Elizabeth's sister."

"Now then Georgie, we mustn't judge others before we have met them," said Lucia, uncomfortably aware that this was exactly what she had been doing.

"It is fun, knowing Elizabeth's little secret,

though, isn't it?" said Georgie. "It almost makes up for the pain of painting Major Benjy's portrait."

TEN

The next day saw Georgie working hard at the portrait of the Major. Despite his feelings regarding the subject, he worked conscientiously at his painting, determined that his efforts, once displayed in public, would not disgrace him.

While taking a break from his paintbrushes, Georgie encountered his model outside the fishmonger's.

"How's it going, Pillson?" demanded the Major. "The portrait, I mean."

"Oh, very well, thank you," said Georgie. In truth, he was more than a little pleased with his efforts. While lacking the sympathy and depth of personal feeling that he had achieved only once before, in his painting of Olga Braceley, the famous *prima donna*, his artistic skills had improved since that time, and he had reason to be contented with his work.

"Excellent," said the Major. "Now if you'll excuse me, I must make a special order."

He ducked into the shop, and, thanks to the Major's customary stentorian tones, Georgie hardly had to strain his ears to catch the order, whatever it might prove to be, for the residents of Grebe. To his astonishment, he heard a demand for four hen lobsters to be delivered on the Thursday morning. It would have taken a far slower brain than Georgie's not to associate the Major's words with the recipe for lobster *à la Riseholme*, which a few years previously had made its way from Lucia's cook's recipe book into Elizabeth Mapp's kitchen by devious means.

"Well," Georgie said to himself, "it does seem as though they are out to impress her sister." He turned to make his way back to Mallards, and impart this news to Lucia, and had only gone a few yards when he collided with Diva Plaistow, who was making her way at great speed in the opposite direction.

"So sorry. Must buy butter for sandwiches.

Paddy ate it all. Sick on kitchen floor. Any news?"

Georgie thought for a second what news it would be acceptable to disseminate. "Lucia and I have received our invitations to the birthday party."

"Me too. *Soirée* indeed! We shall see." Diva sniffed loudly, just as Susan Wyse's Royce swept around the corner.

Susan, clad in her sables, leaned out and called to them. "Algernon and I will be delighted to convey anyone to Grebe on Thursday evening, should they require it."

"Thank you, no," said Georgie. "Most kind of you, but Lucia and I will be driven by Cadman. I was just about to make a similar offer to Mrs Plaistow."

"Oh dear," wailed Diva. "I am sure to offend someone by accepting the other's offer."

"I'm sure Lucia won't be offended if you decide to accept Mrs Wyse's kind offer."

"Nor will Algernon and I be if you travel in Lucia's car."

"This makes it even more difficult," complained Diva.

"I have an idea," said Georgie. "Travel to Grebe with Lucia and me, and accept Mrs Wyse's kind offer to return home."

"What an excellent proposal," Susan called from her sables.

"Oh, you *are* clever," said Diva. "That will be perfect. Thank you. And now the butter. *Au reservoir.*" She scurried off in search of the missing ingredient.

Georgie, now feeling quite proud of his diplomatic skills, wished Susan Wyse a good day, and returned to Mallards.

"I promised that we would take Diva Plaistow to Grebe on Thursday evening. And the Wyses will bring her back into town," he told Lucia on his way up the stairs to his painting. "Oh, and the Major ordered something for the party from Hopkins."

"What? No, don't tell me, let me guess. Lobster?"

"How did you know?" answered Georgie, surprised.

"It would be a poor sort of birthday for Elizabeth if she didn't find some way of attempting to annoy me. Never mind, I will bite my tongue, and my silence will be my birthday present to her."

"We must talk about that," said Georgie. "After I have finished my picture. It's nearly done. I shall show it to you when it's dry."

Georgie was as good as his word. After dinner

that evening, he went upstairs and brought down his portrait of Major Benjamin Mapp-Flint, standing on one of the tees at the golf links, staring down at the small white ball at his feet with an smile of savage intensity.

"Dear me," said Lucia. "You have given him a very powerful expression."

"It's more pleasant than his other smile, believe me," said Georgie.

"But it is him, to the life. If Elizabeth wants a picture of her Benjy, then this will do admirably."

"But if she is expecting a picture of herself...?"

"Then the fault does not lie with you, my dear, but with he who commissioned the picture."

"I hope she sees it that way," Georgie said, miserably.

"She is sure to. Now, let us try that little piece of Mozartino that came the other day."

Georgie, as usual, took the bass part. He had had no time for his usual surreptitious practice, being occupied with his painting, and he missed his entrance three times in a row.

Lucia took off her spectacles, which she had put on to read the music (though she had actually spent some time practicing while Georgie was painting, and hardly needed these aids to vision) and turned to look her husband in the eye.

"Georgino *mio*, is oo tired?"

"Tired and worried," he answered her. "What if the Major doesn't like the picture?"

"Then he will have to 'lump it', in that vulgar phrase of Irene's. Is that all?"

"Elizabeth, of course. I keep wondering what she will have to say about it all."

"That is not your problem, as I said earlier," Lucia assured him. "And what else?"

"You haven't told me what you will be wearing to Elizabeth's party," he said with a frown.

"What of it?"

"We must go as a couple, and I must wear something that complements what you will be wearing. Foljambe hates it if she doesn't have enough time to get my clothes ready."

"Oh, Georgie, is that all?"

"It is a very serious matter," he answered her crossly. "When Foljambe is in a bad mood, life becomes very tarsome. My bath is too hot or too cold, she forgets my hot-water bottle sometimes, and there is never enough starch in my collars."

"Oo poor fing," Lucia cooed. "Well, I have decided what I will wear. Since we are to dine with a Socialist, I will wear the dress that I bought in London that year to attend one of Sophy Alingsby's parties. The green silk."

"That dress?" said Georgie in a tone of great anxiety mixed with embarrassment. "Why, that's the one where the hem is at least an inch above your knees. Isn't that a little daring for Tilling?"

"Nothing ventured, nothing gained," Lucia answered him.

"Well, I don't see what you are going to gain from wearing that," Georgie told her. "But if it is to be green silk, I shall go upstairs and choose my clothes to give to Foljambe."

ELEVEN

The following day, having selected his party outfit with care, and presented it to Foljambe with instructions for its preparation, Georgie was at last settling down to play the piano when Grosvenor informed him that Major Mapp-Flint was downstairs and wished to speak with him.

"Certainly," said Georgie, and took off his spectacles before going downstairs to meet the Major.

"How's it coming along, old boy?" asked the subject of the portrait.

"Oh, it is finished. I was going to tell you that you might collect it. If you'll just wait here, I'll go and bring it down."

When he returned, he found the Major drinking something brown from a glass. "Hope you don't mind, old boy. Your Grosvenor came by to ask if I wanted anything, so I said a whisky and soda would be welcome, as a joke, you understand, and blow me down if she didn't come back the next minute with this. Your health," he added as an afterthought, raising the now empty glass pointedly in Georgie's direction. "Hope you don't mind. Ah, that's it, is it?"

He studied the painting for a while. "I must say that you've caught me in a good pose," he said. "That's excellent work. I knew you were an artist, but I'd only seen your little daubs of the Tilling streets before. This is powerful stuff."

Since he was brandishing his empty glass at this point, it was uncertain whether the Major was referring to the drink or Georgie's painting. Georgie decided that he would take the latter interpretation as he carefully sandwiched the painting between two large pieces of cardboard, which he had brought down together with the portrait.

"But what about the frame?" asked the Major.

"That's for you to decide when you take it to the framer's," Georgie pointed out.

"You mean... I mean... I had assumed that your fee would include the frame."

"Certainly not," said Georgie, more than a little surprised at his own directness.

"Well, I mean to say, old boy, eight guineas is a lot of money, and then to add the cost of a frame to that..."

"I am sorry, Major, but nothing was mentioned about frames. The price for this painting was agreed at eight guineas, if you please."

"Well, if I'm going to have to buy the frame today, I won't have enough money to pay you and the frame shop. And I am not sure that he will let me pay later. So you might have to wait a few days for your guineas."

"I believe the bank is still open," Georgie pointed out, leaving the Major to make the obvious inference. He was amazed at his firmness in standing up to the Major in this way. It was almost as if it were he, and not the Major, who had partaken of a large whisky and soda.

"Oh, very well then." He laboriously counted out seventeen half-sovereigns. "Do you have a florin for change?"

By chance, Georgie happened to have such a coin in his purse, and handed it to the Major, who thanked him, and departed.

Georgie was left standing in the front room,

still astounded at his temerity in the matter of payment, and was so absorbed in his thoughts that he failed to notice Lucia entering.

"Georgino *mio*," she said, and blew him a kiss. "You were *magnifico*!"

"I was? Did you hear us?"

"I heard *tutti* – everything. You stood up to him, and insisted on your money. I was coming down the stairs and listened behind the door until he left. Was that vewy naughty of me?"

"Not at all."

At that moment, the door burst open and Irene Coles fairly tumbled into the hallway. "Sorry I didn't knock, but I simply had to come round and see you."

Lucia said nothing, but merely raised a quizzical eyebrow.

"I had just taken my Primavera to the shop to decide on a frame, when in came old Benjy-Wenjy. And he had a picture with him. And what a picture! Is it yours, Georgie? All by your little self?"

"Yes," Georgie admitted, somewhat embarrassed.

"Did you realise that you are married to an artistic genius, Lucia?"

"You like Georgie's picture of Major Benjy?" Lucia asked.

"Like it? Like it? I love it. I adore it. I've not seen such a brilliant caricature in simply ages. Oh, you are clever, Georgie." And much to Georgie's embarrassment, Irene planted a kiss on his cheek. "I don't usually go around kissing strange men – not that you're strange, Georgie – but I just had to. Oh, I am sorry, you have some blue paint on you now. Not sure how it got from my face onto yours, but don't worry, it suits you."

"I'll go and clean it off," Georgie said, by now rather alarmed at this display of affection from Irene.

"Georgie really is clever, you know," Irene said to Lucia when they were alone. "To capture that expression on old Benjy-Wenjy's face, and to present it in such a way that he didn't realise what an ass he'd made of himself – Benjy is the ass, I mean, not Georgie – that is sheer genius."

"I am not sure that Georgie meant it as a caricature," Lucia told her.

"It doesn't matter," Irene told her blithely. "It is one, and that's really what counts. "When Georgie's washed the paint off and he's all clean and tidy again, just send him round to my place. I'll give him a cocktail or a cup of tea or something and show him some of my new work which no-one has seen yet except for Lucy. He deserves it. Oh, I haven't been so excited since my 'Birth of Venus'. I'm looking forward to the party when Mapp sees the picture for the first time."

"Have you been invited?"

"No, but I wouldn't miss it for simply anything, and even Mapp isn't going to turn me away in front of the other guests, is she?"

Although Lucia had taken advantage of social convention in a similar fashion on several occasions in the past, she was nevertheless taken aback by Irene's directness. "It seems a trifle... unorthodox, dear Irene," she said with a note of disapproval in her voice.

"Who cares?" Irene retorted. "Just send Georgie round, won't you, when he's spick and span again?"

As the door closed behind Irene, Lucia reflected that quaint and amusing as Irene might be at times, and as talented as she would seem to be (though her amount of talent sometimes appeared to others to be more than Lucia would permit her), she reminded Lucia at times of one those faulty hand-grenades in the War of which she had heard, which fizzled and sparked, and sometimes exploded, exposing all around, friend and foe alike, to danger.

When Georgie came downstairs, Lucia relayed Irene's invitation to him.

"Did she really like it?" he asked.

"I'm sure she did," Lucia assured him.

TWELVE

The evening of the party had arrived. No-one in Tilling had seen Elizabeth's sister, though Evie Bartlett claimed to have seen that very morning someone, "very tall and thin, not like Elizabeth at all", dressed in what Evie described as "sensible" clothes, getting into a taxi at the station, which had then sped off in the direction of Grebe.

However, there were several houses, not to mention other settlements, in that direction, and there might be any number of people, tall or short, thin or otherwise, who might have business there. It was noted, though, that neither Elizabeth nor Benjy was to be seen marketing that morning, and though Diva had pointedly followed Withers into Twemlow's, the grocer's, to see if anything could be deduced from her order there, even she could make nothing of an order for two pounds of white flour, and a pound of Cheshire cheese.

Lucia had considered taking a constitutional bicycle ride along the road that led past Grebe, with the possibility of catching a glimpse of whoever might be there, but a series of short sharp showers in the morning, which promised to carry over into the afternoon, put paid to that idea.

Accordingly, at seven o'clock Lucia and Georgie got into the car by which they were to be transported to Grebe by Cadman, calling for Diva at Wasters on the way.

Lucia, as she had said to Georgie earlier, was wearing her green silk dress, which left her knees and a short expanse of leg above them exposed, though covered by stockings. Over this, she was wearing a short bolero jacket, festooned with green glass beads.

Georgie had matched her costume with a few pretty effects of his own, with the foundations comprising a bottle-green velvet smoking jacket and emerald tie. His socks, too, if one cared to look in that direction, were also of the shade that would delight an Irishman, and a ring which held what might have been, but probably was not, a large emerald, adorned his finger.

As Cadman held the door open for Diva to enter the car, she looked with surprise at Lucia's dress.

"I wonder that you can keep warm in that dress, dear," she remarked in tones that were not altogether approving. "I hope that you won't catch cold."

"So sweet of you to think of poor little me," Lucia replied calmly. "I have a blanket for the journey home, dear, since the night promises to be a little chilly."

Diva rapidly changed the subject. "And what a smart outfit, Mr. Georgie," she told him. "Dear me, I feel quite the little mouse tonight."

"No danger of that, Mrs Plaistow," Georgie assured her. "That dress becomes you beautifully."

Diva, accepting the compliment gratefully, simpered and smiled for all of the seven minutes of the journey to Grebe.

Withers opened the door to them, and ushered them into the drawing-room where Elizabeth and Benjy Mapp-Flint stood to receive their first guests of the evening.

"A very happy birthday to you, Elizabeth,"

Georgie said to her, bowing low, and taking her hand as if to kiss it.

"Why, thank you." Elizabeth beamed at her guests, but her face assumed an expression of shock as her gaze fell upon the expanse of Lucia's exposed legs. "My dear, allow me to commiserate with you."

"I beg your pardon?" Lucia answered.

"Your little frock. So sorry it has shrunk in the wash – those cheap fabrics often do, I believe – and that you had nothing else to wear to our little *soirée* this evening. Withers! Please fetch a rug or a blanket for Mrs Pillson, who must be feeling the cold dreadfully."

"Thank you, so kind, but I am perfectly comfortable," Lucia assured her, but if the temperature of the room had matched the tone of her voice as she replied, the inhabitants of the room would have needed to dress like Esquimaux to prevent themselves from freezing to death.

An awkward silence hung over the room, broken by Major Benjy's cough.

"Liz, perhaps you should introduce Catherine to our guests."

"Of course. So sorry, dear." Elizabeth now addressed herself to a tall, slightly eccentrically dressed woman who had been sitting quietly on the sofa, with an expression of amusement slowly spreading over her face. "Diva Plaistow, a very old friend and a Tillingite for many years, and Mr and Mrs Pillson, much more recent additions to our little town. Mrs Pillson was my Mayor when I was Mayoress," she added. "My sister, the Honourable Catherine Sedgewick, MBE, Member of Parliament for Keythorpe."

"Now then, Betty," said the tall woman. "You know how I hate all this business of titles and awards and so on. Please, everybody, I am simply Catherine, Betty's sister." She examined Lucia's face with interest. "I have seen you before, but I don't think we were introduced. It was some years ago, if I remember rightly. Terrace. Westminster. You were taking tea with Garroby-Ashton, who was the Member for Brinton, was he not, the Prime Minister of the day, and another man." She looked at Georgie intently. "But not Mr Pillson, if my memory does not fail me."

"I was with my late husband at that time," Lucia explained. "He died some years ago, and I remarried."

Like the experienced politician that she was, the Member for Keythorpe raced past the unpleasantness with a brief apology in the same way that a motorist dismisses a pedestrian whom he has just soaked from head to toe by driving through a puddle. "Oh, I am sorry to hear that. Have I put my foot in it? Forgive me, please."

"Naturally," smiled Lucia. "But what an amazing memory you must have to be able to remember all those details."

"Exactly like an elephant," smiled Elizabeth, a comparison which appeared to meet with little favour in the eyes of her sister, who appeared somewhat less than delighted at being compared to a pachyderm.

At that moment the door opened, and Withers announced the arrival of Algernon and Susan Wyse. He was dressed, as always, in a slightly old-fashioned style, albeit one of extreme elegance, while Susan, clad in what appeared to be a voluminous lilac satin tent, bore on her chest the decoration that proclaimed her as being a Member of the Order of the British Empire.

"Good evening, Mrs Mapp-Flint, and may I take the liberty of wishing you very many happy returns of the day," Mr Wyse greeted Elizabeth.

"Thank you, Mr Wyse," she replied. "So kind," as she accepted the bunch of flowers which he had been holding behind his back.

"And this is from Georgie and me," Lucia told her, presenting a small package wrapped in red paper which she had been holding until the proper moment presented itself. Unsure as to whether to open it at once and give herself the pleasure of injecting an icy note into her voice as she examined Lucia's gift, or to postpone the pleasure of her scorn until she had a smaller audience of one, but one who would be more likely to agree with her judgement of the gift, that is to say, Major Benjy, Elizabeth took it with a brief word of thanks, and placed it on the table unopened.

Diva presented Elizabeth with a pot of strawberry and rhubarb jam, decorated with a pink ribbon tied in an ornate bow. "Quite the most popular of my jams, my customers tell me," she assured Elizabeth. "I'm sure you will enjoy it."

Elizabeth muttered a brief word of thanks and turned to Mrs Wyse. "Susan, pray meet my sister, Catherine. Catherine, meet Susan and Algernon Wyse, of the Wyses of Whitchurch, two of my oldest friends in Tilling."

Susan was staring at Catherine Sedgewick, who in turn appeared to have her gaze fixed on Susan's considerable *poitrine*.

"Another Member of the Order, I see," said Catherine. "How they love to throw out these little baubles in an attempt to flatter us and to keep us happy and contented."

Susan Wyse, who saw her MBE as the pinnacle of her social career, compared to which all other recognition was as a mess of unleavened bread and bitter herbs, was shocked by the casual nature with which her crowning glory had been dismissed.

"But my dear Mrs Sedgewick..." she began.

"Oh, do please call me Catherine. Any friend of Betty's must be a friend of mine."

"Catherine, then... Do you not feel... I mean to say... Surely..." Somehow it seemed that Susan Wyse was unable to find the words.

"I never wear mine, I'm afraid, except when protocol demands it," Catherine went on, seemingly oblivious of Susan's attempts to defend the honour that had been bestowed on her.

As Catherine's meaning finally sank in, Susan Wyse's confidence visibly collapsed and she appeared, despite the expanse of purple satin, to fade into the background. Happily, everyone's attention was distracted by the arrival of the Padre and Mrs Bartlett, who arrived somewhat wet.

"A wee drappie of rain as we wended our way doon from the town. I ween the weather is turning a bittie dreich." He was clearly in one of his moods when his speech tended to the medieval and North British.

"Our Padre, the Reverend Bartlett," Elizabeth introduced him. "And dear Evie," she added, in a tone that might almost be described as an afterthought.

"Please call me Catherine," said the Member for Keythorpe, introducing herself, and extending her hand to the Padre. "And which part of Scotland do you hail from?"

"Birmingham, actually," he answered, in a quieter voice which hailed from the present day, and well south of the border.

"I see," she answered, in tones that quite clearly indicated that she didn't see at all.

"And a little something to mark the day," squeaked Evie, timidly advancing from behind her husband, and presenting a small package to Elizabeth, who deposited it quietly on a small table to join Lucia and Georgie's gift, Diva's jam, and the Wyses' flowers.

Having entirely forfeited any claim to antiquity or to Scottish heritage, the Padre resumed the conversation in modern English. "Evie and I passed Irene Coles on the way here. She appeared to be making her way to Grebe, but had stopped to sketch something that had caught her eye."

"Irene Coles? The artist?" exclaimed Catherine. "I had heard that she lives in Tilling. I would very much like to meet the artist who painted that superb Picture of the Year of you and your husband some years ago. Is she a close friend of yours, Betty?"

"A most dear friend," Elizabeth replied without blushing. "I received no reply to my invitation, so I am afraid that she may not be coming."

Elizabeth's hopes of avoiding any awkwardness and embarrassment were dashed as the door was flung open, and Irene burst in. "Dear sweet one," she cooed to Elizabeth, in tones that reminded all those present, including Elizabeth Mapp-Flint herself, of Elizabeth's own honey-coated vinegar. "How kind of you to let me share the celebration of your coming of age. I didn't get an invitation, but never mind. Heigh-ho, sez she, and we'll all be happy together! Oh, so this is your sister, the famous Catherine Mapp, I believe?"

Elizabeth felt it more tactful to ignore the tone of this speech, and all the content other than the last sentence, and hastened to introduce Irene and Catherine.

"'Famous', you say?" said Catherine to Irene. "How very flattering from one who has herself achieved such fame at a young age."

"I'm older than you were when you set fire to the contents of the pillar-boxes in Whitehall and Downing Street," replied Irene. "Jolly brave of you."

"We all do things in our youth," Catherine told her, "about which we have second thoughts later on. Surely you feel that with your paintings? The picture of Betty and Ben," she indicated Elizabeth and Major Benjy, "that caused such a stir at the Academy the other year?"

"Oh, that," Irene scoffed. "I'm much better now. Come round and see what I'm up to some time soon. Benjy-wenjy, old boy, is that a drink in your hand that you're about to give me? *Quai-hai!*"

During all this time Major Benjy had been circulating among the guests, a jug of the economical wine cup in one hand, and a glass in the other. He was taking great care to keep everyone's glass filled, including his own, which seemed to empty more rapidly than anyone else's. It could be noticed, however, that while he seemed careless of his position whenever he attended to others' glasses, he took great care to turn his back on Elizabeth when refilling his own, to which he added a surreptitious dose of a brown liquid from a hip-flask which was hurriedly replaced in his back pocket.

Irene, a large glass of cup in her hand, raised her glass. "To Elizabeth Mapp-Flint and all who sail in her!" she proclaimed loudly, and drained her drink at one go.

There was a faint confused echo from the other guests, who felt that they should toast their hostess, but found Irene's wording to be best described by the adjective that usually characterised Irene herself – that is to say, 'quaint'.

Major Benjy, however, had followed Irene's lead in the matter of drinking, and echoed the toast with a loud "God bless her!" which dropped loudly into the silence.

"Thank you, dear," Elizabeth said to Irene, in a tone that dripped with irony. "And since we have all finished our drinks, have we not, perhaps we may take our places at the table."

It may or may not have been a coincidence (and Lucia, for one, did not consider it one) that Elizabeth's comment about the drinks came immediately after she had caught sight of the hip-flask that Major Benjy had absent-mindedly placed in full view on the sideboard, in his enthusiasm at joining Irene's toast.

The party trooped into the dining-room, where the first course consisted of a pale warm liquid which at some time had been in close proximity to some fungi, and passed itself off as mushroom soup. This was accompanied by some limp toast, and a light and somewhat sour hock, and was consumed in near-silence.

THIRTEEN

Next, Withers brought in a dish, the aroma emanating from which was all too familiar to Lucia and Georgie, and was swiftly recognised by the others, if the change in expression on their faces was a reliable guide. No-one dared to compliment Elizabeth on her production of lobster *à la Riseholme*, for no-one could forget how the recipe had been acquired from this kitchen, from the time when Lucia had lived in this very house, on the day of the great flood that had swept the two ladies out to sea?

No-one, that is, except Elizabeth's sister, who, Judas-like, betrayed one to whom she was supposedly close. "A wonderful dish, Betty," she exclaimed, when she had tasted and marvelled. "You must give me the recipe."

Elizabeth was prevented from replying by a small explosion from the other end of the table, where Irene, whose place had been hastily laid for her, seemed to be suffering from an acute attack of hiccoughs. The Padre was discreetly patting her on the back as she sipped from a glass of water, explaining that a crumb had gone down the wrong way.

Irene's convulsions ceased at last, and she raised her head to fix Elizabeth with an expression that to the unknowing might have appeared innocent, but to Elizabeth appeared to be the gaze of a Gorgon. Under that look, she could only stammer out a few inconsequential words to her sister, at which Georgie and Lucia exchanged meaningful glances, but held their peace.

The Padre, covering the awkward silence that ensued, burst out with, "'Twill be a bonny day tomorrow, methinks," entirely forgetting that he had been exposed as being neither Scotch nor of the Middle Ages.

"A promise of rain in the afternoon, I heard," Mr Wyse replied.

"A wee drappie will do no harm. Now if it were the same as those floods at Christmas a few years back—" He stopped, acutely aware, as were almost all around the table, of the circumstances surrounding those floods, so intimately linked with the recipe for the dish they were all enjoying.

"Ah yes, those floods," Catherine remarked. "You had an incredible adventure, did you not, Betty? I seem to recall that you were not alone on your voyage?"

"Yes, I was able to comfort Mrs Pillson, or Mrs Lucas as she was then, as we floated out to sea on the table, which is still in my kitchen."

"After such trials together, you must be the closest of friends now," Catherine said, a remark that prompted another bout of coughing and hiccoughs from Irene.

"Irene, dear," said Lucia, her lips set in a firm line, "may I be of assistance?" She rose from her seat, and deftly steered Irene out of the room. "Just wait till we come back," she told the assembled guests, all except one of whom recalled these words as being having been used by Lucia on a previous occasion.

Once outside the door, Irene turned to Lucia with a face where sadness and anger appeared to be equally mixed.

"You're an angel, Lucia. How can you sit there and listen to Mapp's poisonous lies without saying anything to her? I was about to call her out on her pettiness and meanness."

"I know you were, dear," Lucia told her. "But it is the poor thing's birthday party. Her little jibes and taunts give her so much pleasure, and don't bother me in the slightest."

"Dearest!" exclaimed Irene, and kissed her. "But don't you feel just a little annoyed?"

"I cannot let myself sink to her level," said Lucia, giving her silvery laugh, but her eyes told a somewhat different story. "Now when we go back and join the others, Irene dear, please don't make an exhibition of yourself. Let us all enjoy our lobster – that, at least, was properly prepared and served—"

"As well it should be," Irene commented bitterly.

"Now, now, no rancour. Come." She took Irene gently, but firmly, by the elbow, and they re-entered the room together.

"I trust that dearest Lulu has cured you of your cough, or whatever it was that was troubling you?" Elizabeth enquired solicitously.

"Thank you, dear Liblib," Irene replied in sugared tones. "I am much better now."

"Oh, is that the name you go by now, Betty?" her sister enquired. "I see I must adapt myself to local custom and start calling you by that name."

"That will be nice, dear," Elizabeth answered, a look of black fury passing momentarily over her face. "More lobster?"

Alas, there was none left in the dish. Major Benjy, being the last to be served, had taken all that had remained.

"Never mind. I am sure you will give me the recipe. It will do very nicely for my next dinner-party with the Home Secretary and the Lord Chancellor."

Despite the repeated unfortunate gaffes, the whole table was entranced and felt itself ennobled by being privileged to mix in such exalted company, albeit at second-hand. Even Lucia, who had frequently been heard to say that she believed (though alas, her actions at times appeared to speak of a lack of firm belief in this principle) that worldly wealth and position meant nothing to her, appeared visibly impressed.

As for Elizabeth, who should have been the heroine of the hour, she was as a flickering candle beside the blinding searchlight of her sister. To her credit, Catherine quickly spotted this with her experienced politician's eye, and made a brief and polished speech in which she talked with affection of the times that she and her sister had spent in Tilling, and the remarkable talents in the field of painting and other forms of artistic and social endeavour that Elizabeth had shown from an early age. It was done with such skill and tact that no-one present, other than perhaps the subject of the encomium herself, found it possible to raise even the slightest inward cavil, and at the end, when Catherine proposed a toast to her sister, all glasses of the thin liquid presenting itself as hock were raised with such apparent sincerity that even her sister displayed her splendid teeth in a crocodile smile.

After the dessert, a mess of meringue in custard with a spoonful of jam on top, which Elizabeth proudly announced as "floating islands" ("*isole galleggianti*", Lucia translated for Georgie's benefit), Major Benjy stood and rapped his glass.

"Our mosht dish-tingished guesht, Ladiesh and Genglemen," he began, and then stopped, seemingly unsure as to how to proceed. "We are all of us gathered here today to shelebrate the anniversary of a very special lady to whom I have the honour to be attached and tied, which is to say, not putting too fine a point on it, my very dear wife, Liz. Her birthday which was, as you may or may not know, but it doeshn't really matter if you do or not, because..." Here he tailed off again, and, to the visible dismay of Susan Wyse, who was sitting to his left, swayed like a tall poplar in a powerful wind. Just as it appeared that he was about to lose his balance completely, he steadied himself by clutching at the tablecloth, and restarted his oration. "It was many yearsh ago that Elizabeth Mapp made an appearansh in thish world. And it gives me great privilege to have the pleasure of being the honour of becoming her wife a few yearsh ago."

The Padre, who was to his right, gave a surreptitious tug at the back of the Major's dinner-jacket, well aware that all was not as it should be in the Major's mind, in an attempt to slow the wine-inspired flow. For his part, the Major, resenting this interruption, whirled around, a look of ferocity on his face, and seemed to be about to strike the Padre before stopping himself abruptly. However, these sudden movements appeared to upset his balance, and he was forced to clutch once more at the tablecloth to support himself, but this time with a more deleterious effect than before, resulting in the remains of a dish of floating islands landing in the Padre's lap.

"Benjy-boy, my dear," Elizabeth smiled through clenched teeth. "Thank you for your lovely words. I am sure we have all heard enough for now. Ladies, shall we leave the gentlemen? Padre, I shall send Withers to attend to you. So sorry. Mr Wyse, I rely on you not to keep us waiting too long."

She swept out of the room, followed by (in that order), her sister Catherine, Susan Wyse, Diva, Irene, Evie, and Lucia, who gave Georgie a surreptitious wink as she left the room.

After Withers had appeared and departed with a cloth and towel with which the Padre set about cleaning his trousers, there was silence from the four men seated around the dining table, with the Major shaking his head sadly. "What happened?" he kept asking, but no-one seemed inclined to give him an answer.

"Where'sh the port?" he asked at length, but no-one seemed to be able to find it. "'Straordinary thing, but it was here, I could have sworn," the Major informed them all. Georgie was probably the only one who failed to share the Major's bafflement, as he had seen Elizabeth's sister discreetly and tactfully remove the decanter from its place on the sideboard behind Benjy, doubtless to spare her sister Elizabeth further embarrassment.

"Tell you all what, though," the Major told the company, attempting and failing to light a small cigar. "I've got a present for Liz. *He* knows all about it," pointing at Georgie, "but he's not to tell. Mum's the word, eh, old man?"

"Time we joined the ladies," Mr Wyse announced emphatically, after a stunned silence of about thirty seconds had greeted Major Benjy's latest pronouncement.

"Quite right, quite right. Won't do to keep Liz waiting, especially on her birthday."

FOURTEEN

"**G**ot something for you, Liz," the Major announced as the small party of men entered the room.

"That's nice, dear," Elizabeth answered him, in an icy tone which would have closed the door firmly on any attempt to continue the discussion, had it been addressed to anyone in full command of their senses. However, Major Benjy's senses were clearly elsewhere, and so far from his being in command of them, they would appear to have mutinied and deserted.

"It's here," he announced, bending to pick something from behind one of the sofas. He staggered, and was prevented from falling by the Padre, who caught at his arm and steadied him. As he stood, it could be seen that in his hand was a flat package, the size of a large thin book, that appeared to have been hastily wrapped in brown paper.

"Happy Birthday, Liz," Benjy said to his wife, thrusting the package into her hand before collapsing into an armchair.

Elizabeth swiftly calculated that it would appear churlish to ignore her husband's gift. "Thank you, Benjy-boy," she said in the same sweetly acid tones as she had used previously, and started to unwrap it.

The surprise on her face as Georgie's painting was revealed lasted for an almost, but not quite, imperceptibly short time. "How lovely, dear," she told the by now somnolent Benjy.

"May we see, dear?" sweetly enquired Lucia.

With a look almost of disgust, Elizabeth turned the painting around, exposing it to the view of the assembled company.

The portrait was now in a handsome gilt frame, which even Georgie had to admit, enhanced the picture. Major Benjy was depicted holding a golf-club with an expression of a kind that was probably intended to be a friendly smile, but to some onlookers rather resembled the snarl of one of the tigers that he had hunted in the Indian jungle. This was in no way due to a lack of skill on Georgie's part, as this was an expression that often adorned the Major's features.

"How powerful!" exclaimed Mr Wyse, almost recoiling from Major Benjy's snarling tiger-like smile.

"And how lifelike!" squeaked Evie. "It is him to the life!"

"Who can have painted it?" Susan wondered aloud. "Dear Irene, I am sure it was you?"

Irene gave a less than elegant shrug, saying, "Hardly my style, dear Susan," in a voice that could hardly be acquitted of mimicry. She half-turned in Georgie's direction, and gave a wink unmistakably aimed at him.

"Well, I wonder who could have painted it, then?" Elizabeth enquired, fixing Lucia with a steely gaze.

"My dear Elizabeth, you know my poor little daubs," Lucia told her. "They are hardly up to the standard of this little masterpiece. I must assure you most categorically that I had nothing to do with its production."

If Benjy had been in any state to listen to her, and if they had been alone, Elizabeth would have had many words to say about this denial. As it was, she had to content herself with a mere sniff of disdain, but it was a sniff that said more than many words might have done.

"Well, it's a jolly nice picture of your Ben, Betty," Catherine consoled her sister. "And it must have cost him a pretty penny, I must say. One of my colleagues had his portrait painted recently, and I believe he paid over one hundred guineas for it—"

"—and if the artist was any good, he got a bargain there," Irene interrupted her.

"Absolutely. Just what I was going to say," Catherine added, with the diplomacy of an experienced politician. "I must say, I am looking forward to seeing your studio and your work."

Irene positively simpered, a thing never before seen in Tilling. "You are always most welcome."

Meanwhile, Lucia had been edging closer to the boudoir grand piano that stood in the corner of the room, and uttered an exclamation of surprise.

"This is not your Aunt Caroline's Blumenfelt!"

"No, dear. When we moved here from dear Aunt Caroline's house, I discovered that the last tenant of Mallards had completely destroyed its tone by moving it into the telephone-room. I was therefore forced to replace it with this. A most inferior instrument, but since my investments in the City are not delivering what I expected, then needs must, alas."

Since the last tenant of Mallards had been Lucia, who had then manoeuvred her way into the possession of the ancestral house, and had also unwittingly led Elizabeth into a number of unwise financial speculations, this little speech contained the makings of a fierce quarrel that could keep Tilling entertained for at least a week.

It was a sad disappointment to many in the room that Lucia refused to rise to the challenge. "I wonder you did not charge the tenant for dilapidations," she answered sweetly.

"By the time I discovered the true extent of the damage, it was too late." It was a poor riposte, and Lucia magnanimously decided not to push the point further.

"The lid appears to be locked," she stated, after attempting to open it. Might I trouble you for the key? I would dearly appreciate the honour of running my fingers over the keys."

Elizabeth, who had hoped that Lucia would make a request to regale the company with her rendering of the slow movement of Beethoven's "Moonlight" sonata, and was anticipating with pleasure her refusal of the request, was prepared for this.

"Ah yes. So sorry, dear. Benjy-boy was playing on the piano the other day, and must have absent-mindedly slipped the key into his waistcoat pocket. And now, poor boy, he is asleep. Worn out after a long morning on the links, and I don't have the heart to wake him. So sorry, dear. Maybe another time?"

The assembled company metaphorically licked its lips, and strained forward, somewhat in the manner of ancient Romans watching gladiators in the amphitheatre. However, their expectations were dashed, when Lucia, who knew full well that Major Benjamin Mapp-Flint had the musical sensibilities of a somewhat deaf rhinoceros, was not fooled for a minute by Elizabeth's answer, and simply replied, "So sad, dear. Another time, certainly."

Smiles, indicating that the skirmish was now at a temporary standstill, were exchanged, and the guests drew round the painting once again to examine it. Georgie felt it unwise not to join the throng, and his vanity (for vanity was a vice from which he suffered, albeit chiefly in the matter of appearance and dress) urged him to hear what others thought of the anonymous artist's work.

To his intense pleasure, and some embarrassment, he heard nothing but praise for the anonymous genius who had created this masterpiece.

After such expressions of appreciation, there was nothing for Elizabeth to do but to accept the compliments gracefully, and to smile as winningly as possible under the circumstances. Her desire to see her guests depart was noticeable, though, and they tactfully took the unspoken hints that emanated from her.

The thanks and goodnights were addressed solely to the hostess of the party, the host still reclining, seemingly comatose, in his armchair. Only when the guests had departed did Elizabeth remember her birthday cake, which was resting, forgotten and untasted, in the kitchen. If she had been a duchess or even a member of the minor nobility, she would have sworn like a sailor, but her upbringing forbade such vulgarity. Instead, she stumped off to bed, leaving her husband downstairs, snoring peacefully.

The Wyses, as arranged, provided Diva with a ride back to Tilling, and, seeing the Padre and Evie preparing to walk back, Susan very generously made room in the Royce for them as well. For their part, Lucia and Georgie invited Irene to share their car.

FIFTEEN

As soon as they started off from Grebe, Irene burst into hoots of laughter.

"Oh, it's all too priceless," she gasped between guffaws. "Mapp having to pretend she liked your picture, Georgie!"

"Yes, well, it is quite a good likeness," Georgie replied, somewhat stiffly.

"Oh no, that's not what I meant. Yes, in its way it's a very good picture, but don't tell the Academy I said that, because they're all meant to be frightfully keen on people like your friend Tancred Sigismund who you told me about, Lucia. By the way, I met him once in London, and he was drunk and kept trying to kiss me.

Ugh!" She shuddered. "Did he try to kiss you, Lucia?"

"Certainly not!" Lucia answered indignantly.

"Don't get on your high horse, dear. I was only teasing. No, what Mapp's so furious about is what you told me, Georgie. She wanted a portrait of herself, and Benjy-boy gave her one of himself. And that smile!" She collapsed against the seat of the car in a fit of helpless giggling. "Oh, you really have done it now, Georgie."

The car slowed to a halt outside Taormina, Irene's house. "Here we are," said Lucia. "Goodnight, dear, and do take care."

"Don't you worry about me," said Irene. "Lucy will see me to bed. Or would you like to come in for a nightcap?"

"Thank you, dear, but some other time perhaps," Lucia told her.

"Which means never. But anyway – off to bed I go. A jolly good evening, don't you think?"

To this, there was no obvious answer, and Lucia did not feel inclined to provide one.

"Poor Elizabeth," she sighed to Georgie as they entered the house together. " She tries so hard, poor thing, and everything seems to go against her."

"I don't feel sorry for her in the least. She was perfectly horrid to everyone. Just because it was her birthday doesn't mean she can be rude to you, and ignore your and Diva's presents and the Padre's."

"I suppose you are right. What did you make of her sister?"

"She's interesting. A little frightening, with that memory. How she remembered you taking tea on the House of Commons Terrace with the Prime Minister."

"Of course, I remember it perfectly," said Lucia. "It was such a treat for poor Pepino. But for her to remember it after so long – I agree. It is quite remarkable, is it not?"

They went upstairs and were just about to enter their separate bedrooms, when Georgie called out, "The cake!"

"Sorry, darling?"

"Elizabeth's birthday cake. Major Benjy told me that she had ordered a special cake for her birthday, and there was no sign of it just now."

"Perhaps she cancelled it. It would be just like her to save a few pennies here and there, even for her own birthday party."

"Or perhaps she was so upset at Benjy's present to her that she forgot about it, or decided to go without."

"You may be right, Georgie. In fact, thinking

about it, I am sure you have found the true solution. *Buona notte.*"

"And to you."

Sixteen

Georgie and Lucia were eating their breakfast the next morning when Grosvenor entered to announce the arrival of a visitor.

"A Mrs Catherine Sedgewick, madam."

"Elizabeth's sister? At this hour? Show her in."

"How exciting!" said Georgie. "What on earth do you think it's all about?"

Lucia was spared from answering by the entrance of Catherine Sedgewick, who apologised profusely for the interruption.

"Not at all," Lucia assured her. "Please, take a seat. Some coffee? Have you breakfasted? Some toast? Fig preserve from the tree in the garden?"

"Thank you, I will," Catherine answered her. "Please do forgive me," she repeated. "I am well aware that you hardly know me from Adam, and *vice versa*, of course, but other than Betty, your address is the only one I know in Tilling – Aunt Caroline, of course."

"But... but..." Georgie broke off, unsure how to phrase the question.

"But why am I not at Grebe?" Catherine rescued him from his floundering. "I am not at Grebe, Mr Pillson, because my termagant of a sister and that drunken sot of a husband of hers have made life unbearable there. The argument started, as far as I am aware, at three this morning, presumably when the Major woke up and found himself alone in his chair before stumbling noisily upstairs, waking me, and Betty, who screamed at him using terms and language more appropriate to a fishwife. In fact, I have come into contact with many fishwives in my time, and they were perfect ladies compared to what I heard." She paused and took a bite of toast and a sip of coffee.

"Do go on," said Georgie greedily.

"It's nice to have an appreciative audience," she smiled. "I put my pillow over my head and attempted to get some sleep, but the noise went on for hours. It always did, when we were girls together. Betty would never bury a hatchet as long as she was capable of waving it in her opponent's face.

"So I slipped out of the house at the earliest hour one could consider decent, and made my way to the only other house in Tilling that I know. Thank you very much for welcoming the stranger at your gates."

"The least we could do," Lucia told her.

"Now, I know that this will sound like a terrible imposition, and if you say no, I shall remove myself to the Trader's Arms. When I accepted my sister's invitation to come and stay here for a week on account of her birthday, I saw it as a golden opportunity to have my house redecorated and refurbished. I therefore have no home to go back to if I remove myself from Grebe. So, hesitant as I am—"

Lucia immediately grasped the import of this speech and burst in with, "I take it that you would like to stay here for a few days, refreshing your memories of childhood? Georgie and I would be delighted to have you as our guest, wouldn't we, Georgie?"

"Most certainly we would," Georgie agreed enthusiastically. "May we ask when you last stayed here?"

"More years ago than I care to admit," she

laughed. "However, I did come to visit Betty some five or six years ago, and I was saddened to see how much she had let the place go to what I can only describe as rack and ruin. I do approve of all the changes I have seen so far, though. And I do so want to see the garden again. It holds many happy memories."

"With pleasure," said Lucia. Her pleasure at the thought of having a Member of Parliament (one, moreover who was noted in *Who's Who* for sensational political activities) under her roof was only matched by that excited by the thought of stealing Elizabeth's sister from under her very nose (though she would never have expressed it in those terms).

Following breakfast, Catherine was dispatched, together with Cadman and Foljambe, to pack and remove all her effects from Grebe. She and Lucia had already chosen the room in which she was to sleep, which by a happy coincidence was the room in which she had stayed when visiting her aunt as a girl.

"I would like to hear that conversation between her and Elizabeth," Georgie said.

"Now then, we mustn't be greedy," Lucia told him. "No doubt we will receive full accounts, from both sides, in due course."

An hour and a half after she had set off,

Catherine returned with two small cases and a portmanteau.

"I can't begin to tell you how grateful I am," she said to Lucia, after Cadman had heaved her luggage up the stairs, and Foljambe (who had been very generously "shared" with Catherine by Georgie) had started unpacking. "The atmosphere in that place is poisonous, more poisonous than anything I have ever seen in the House. When I left this morning, she seemed about to throw the contents of the crockery-cabinet at him, from what I could hear."

"No!" said Georgie.

"Not that she would ever do anything like that, though. She's far too careful with the pennies to try a trick like that. Always has been, ever since I can remember. Why, she used to let out this lovely old house to holidaymakers every summer."

"And very glad I am that she did so," said Lucia hastily, before Catherine could start expounding on the moral and other deficiencies of these holidaymakers. "I took Mallards for the summer some years ago, and I fell so in love with Tilling that I could not bear to tear myself away."

"And you, Mr Pillson? Were you so in love that you could not tear yourself away, either?"

Georgie blushed to the roots of his hair, unsure of the identity of the object of his implied affections to which Catherine was alluding, and stammered that he had found Tilling so charming, and that he and Lucia had been friends for so long that he too had decided to move from Riseholme. Happily, Catherine did not press the point, but tactfully changed the subject.

"And you were elected Mayor of Tilling?" she asked Lucia. "Congratulations."

Though Lucia was indeed extremely proud of the fact that she had been Mayor of Tilling for a year, she had sufficient perception to realise that this was as nothing when compared to the exploits of Catherine Sedgewick (*née* Mapp) in the political sphere and that any attempts at competition in that arena were doomed to failure before they were even begun.

"Chiefly a ceremonial role, I fear," she said, surprising Georgie, who had memories of the garden-room being filled with tin boxes marked "Housing", "Markets", "Roads" and the like and Lucia's constant protestations regarding the incessant press of official business. "But it was a great honour."

"Indeed. And Betty was your Mayoress."

"She was. She did her best to support me."

"And support herself as well, pushing herself to a position above the Mayor, if I know my sister."

Catherine glanced at the portrait of the Mayor that had been painted by Irene, showing her in Mayoral robes, with her bicycle, piano, and a pack of cards. "That is a Coles, if I am not mistaken. A very Mannerist subject in a powerful modern style. Why is it not in the Town Hall where it clearly belongs?"

"Alas, the Committee rejected its placement there."

"And I may guess who chaired the Committee. So like her. And, while we are on the subject of portraits, whose creation is that picture of the Major? That is not Coles' work, I am sure. Those charming watercolours I see on the wall? May I guess that they are yours?"

"Indeed they are," said Lucia, struck by the contrast between Elizabeth's sister and Elizabeth herself in the matter of artistic appreciation.

"But this," Catherine went on, indicating the portrait of Lucia at the piano that Georgie had given to her as a Christmas present some years earlier. "This is surely the work of the unknown master or mistress who captured the Major's expression so well."

Again, Georgie blushed. Catherine noticed and continued, "I trust that he paid you well for your work? No, don't bother to answer that. Never mind, it is a fine piece of painting. Now, Mrs Pillson—"

"Oh, please call me Lucia."

"Thank you. Very well then, Lucia, may I go into the garden?"

"Of course? May I escort you, or would you prefer to revive your memories alone?"

"If you would be so kind as to accompany me, I would be delighted."

As the pair left the room, Georgie basked in the glow that accompanies the recognition of one's artistic talents.

SEVENTEEN

No such sense of contentment reigned at Grebe. As Elizabeth's sister had correctly deduced, Major Benjy had awakened in the night, and found himself, somewhat to his surprise, in his armchair. The lights and the fire had gone out, and the room was distinctly chilly.

Rubbing his eyes, he had endeavoured to remember what events might have led up to this situation, and had a vague memory of presenting his portrait to Elizabeth, but try as he might, he was unable to recall her reaction.

On attempting to rise, his aching head reminded him painfully of the whisky he had surreptitiously slipped into the wine cup that had been served before the meal, and the sour hock with which he had so frequently replenished his glass during dinner.

On the principle of "the hair of the dog", he groped painfully for the hip-flask which he remembered was in the pocket of his dinner-jacket, but to his astonishment it was empty.

"Most strange," he told himself. With an effort, he heaved himself out of the chair, and started to stumble his way upstairs.

As he tripped for the third time, the bedroom door was flung open, and Elizabeth stood there, arms akimbo and eyes which seemed to dart fire. Like one who has gazed on a basilisk, the Major seemed turned to stone, and he froze in mid-step.

"Benjamin Mapp-Flint, I will not have you coming into this room. Your disgusting inebriated antics which completely ruined the little *soirée* I had intended for my friends have made you a stranger to me. You may sleep in the back bedroom in the future, since my sister is occupying the guest room. You will find your things in there ready for you. Now, get in there!"

"But Liz..." he began weakly.

"Don't you dare 'Liz' me, you drunken sot!" she fairly screamed at him. "From now on, you will address me as 'Elizabeth'. And I shall expect a full apology for your behaviour in the morning, when you are in a fit state to deliver one."

"But... but..." The bedroom door slammed shut, and the Major was left alone, cold and disconsolate, halfway through his journey. Sadly, he resumed his ascent of the stairs, which now seemed to him to be as steep and arduous as the north face of the Matterhorn, and half-stumbled, half-crawled to the meanly furnished room which was to be his resting-place for the night, and where, as promised, many of his "necessaries" were awaiting his arrival.

He removed his boots and his dinner-jacket before flinging himself on the bed, but he had hardly closed his eyes when he was disturbed by his wife's voice screaming what was probably abuse, had he taken the trouble to listen to it. At length it stopped, and he drifted into some sort of dozing sleep, only to be awakened what seemed like minutes later by the sound of loud sobbing, interspersed with more shrieks of apparent abuse. This continued for what remained of the night as he lay wretchedly waiting for the dawn.

At length he heard the sounds of Elizabeth arising and then making her way downstairs. As stealthily as he dared, he opened the door and crept to the bathroom, where he washed and shaved before tiptoeing his way into the bedroom which he shared with Elizabeth, and chose a clean collar and shirt.

His head still throbbed, but he knew better than to expect any kind of sympathy when he went downstairs to confront his wife.

Nor were his predictions in error, as he swiftly discovered.

"I should hope you are ashamed of yourself," was her cold greeting to him, delivered at full volume over a bowl of porridge. "My birthday party was ruined by your unspeakably boorish behaviour last night."

The Major, who by now was beginning to feel that a small steel foundry had started operations inside his skull, could only mumble an incoherent apology.

"And the cake!" shouted Elizabeth.

"What cake?" he asked, completely taken aback.

"My birthday cake, you drunken fool! If you remember, there was to be a birthday cake, with fifty-two candles, and no-one even saw it, let alone tasted it, thanks to you and your devious underhanded ways."

This accusation stung Major Benjy to the quick, and despite the steam hammers and rolling mills at work around his brain, and the general feeling of malaise that infected him from head (especially) to toe, he felt impelled to defend himself. "No-one," he said, as forcefully as his aching head would permit, and shaking a warning finger at her. "No-one calls Major Benjamin Flint or Mapp-Flint or whoever he may be, late of his Majesty's Indian Army, devious or underhanded. No-one."

The effort of making this speech appeared to leave him quite drained of energy, and he sank into a chair.

"Then what do you call it," Elizabeth answered him, her voice rising to a piercing shriek, "when you hide a flask of whisky in your pocket, and fill your glass with whisky whenever you believe that no-one is watching you? If that's not devious and underhanded, then I don't know the meaning of the word."

"It's two words. Devious and underhanded," he pointed out, the spirits of grammatical logic overpowering those of common-sense, who would have advised him to hold his tongue on the subject.

"I can count, thank you very much!"

At this point Withers appeared in the doorway with a plate of eggs and bacon for Elizabeth, but on beholding the scene between the couple, made a swift exit, bearing the food away with her.

"And," Elizabeth continued, hardly stopping to draw breath, "what on earth did you mean by your reply to Irene's absurd toast?"

But this was a question which was beyond the capabilities of the Major to answer at this time. His head sank on his breast, and he closed his eyes.

"Wake up!" Elizabeth fairly screamed at him. "Open your eyes and look at me when I am talking to you!" He did so, seeing in his wife's expression the face of a High Court judge who has just heard the jury pronounce a verdict of "Guilty" on a prisoner accused of a particularly heinous crime, and whose pleasurable duty it is now to pass sentence.

The black cap went on. "And the portrait! Why on earth did you decide that a picture of your miserable self would be a suitable present for me on my fiftieth birthday? Eh?"

"I... Er... Well... I thought that's what you wanted."

"You fool! Why would anyone in their senses want a picture of *you* to hang on their wall?"

Much too late, daylight dawned in Major Benjy's mind as he realised his blunder. "You mean... you were asking me for a portrait of yourself?"

"Of course I did! Why Lucia has that portrait of herself by Irene which the Council decided was not to hang in the Town Hall, and there's that other one of her playing the piano by Georgie. Why shouldn't I have a portrait of myself?"

At this point, her harangue was replaced by a series of distressed sniffs as she dabbed her dry eyes with a handkerchief, concealing the fact that no tears were flowing. In the relative silence, the front door could be heard opening and closing.

"Who can that be?" Elizabeth asked, and, handkerchief and imaginary tears forgotten, crossed to the window. "Why, it's Catherine, hurrying down the road towards the town! What can she be doing?" She turned to her husband. "Run after her and find out!"

Benjy was at first inclined to argue, but one look at Elizabeth's face changed his mind. He heaved himself to his feet, and set off gamely in pursuit of his sister-in-law who, however, seemed to be moving faster than he could manage, and he was compelled to give up the chase, winded, after only a hundred yards or so.

"Sorry," he panted. "She was too fast for me."

"So I observed," Elizabeth said acidly. "Never mind. I am sure we will discover soon enough when she comes back."

In the shared curiosity regarding Catherine's destination, hostilities between the Mapp-Flints temporarily ceased, and Elizabeth thawed enough to pour a cup of tea for her husband.

"Thank you," he said as he took it. "And I wish to apologise most sincerely for my behaviour last night. I don't know what came over me."

The volcano was not extinct, but merely dormant. "I know very well what it was," Elizabeth replied sternly. "And so do you."

"Yes, well." He clutched his head in his hands. "'Pon my word, I am ashamed of myself this morning."

"And that picture of you, what are we to do with it? I never want to see it again. It will always remind me of that terrible evening."

"It cost a pretty penny, I can tell you," Benjy told her. "Far too much for it to be thrown out."

"Then I will return it to you, and you can then find a place to hang it where I will never see it. Your dressing-room, perhaps?"

"Or I might present it to the golf club?" Benjy suggested. "The gift of a portrait of one of their more distinguished members would hardly go amiss, I feel."

There was an expectant pause in the conversation, which by now had returned to an almost civilised level, during which Elizabeth's gaze was fixed on the sideboard.

Benjy followed the direction of her eyes, and saw a number of unfamiliar objects there. With an almost superhuman effort of concentration, he forced himself into making the logical connection between these objects, which he by now had deduced as being the gifts presented to Elizabeth the previous evening, and the present conversation.

"And... and of course I would also commission your portrait as your birthday present. To be hung in this room, of course."

Elizabeth, pleased that she had finally managed to steer her husband's thoughts in the right direction, relaxed a little.

"And I am sure you have determined who you would ask to paint it. After Irene's triumph at the Royal Academy, there really cannot be any question, can there?"

The fee that Irene had demanded danced before the Major's eyes, and he recalled it, when compared to his slender bank balance, with horror. "Of course," he said, wondering how he was going to manage to fulfil this request.

Peace of a kind now appeared to reign, and Withers felt emboldened enough to reappear with eggs and bacon for two.

After breakfast, which was eaten in a wary silence, Elizabeth rose, and looked out of the window.

"Isn't that Lucia's Royce coming down the road? I wonder what she has forgotten."

Major Benjy joined her at the window. "By Jove, you're right, Liz! That's that chauffeur of hers – Cadman, isn't it? And his wife, Pillson's maid with the fancy French name."

"Foljambe, yes. And that's— no, it can't be. Yes it is. It's my sister Catherine in the back. Well!"

"What on earth is she doing in that car?" Benjy asked.

"We will find out soon enough."

Catherine imparted the news of her removal to her sister, and there was much wailing and metaphorical gnashing of Elizabeth's fine set of teeth.

"But why, Catherine?" she asked for the tenth time in as many minutes.

"I do not feel under any compulsion to answer that question," Catherine answered, taking some of her clothes out of a drawer, and passing them to Foljambe, who folded them neatly before stowing them in a portmanteau.

"I call it most ungrateful," Elizabeth complained. "And from my own sister, as well."

"You may call it whatever you please," Catherine answered her. "And a fine sister you were, when it came to Aunt Caroline's will."

Elizabeth opened her mouth very wide, and then shut it again, clearly having decided that under the circumstances, silence was the best policy.

"I am sure we shall meet in town over the next few days," Catherine said in farewell, as Foljambe closed the portmanteau and called for Cadman to transport it down the stairs.

There was no reply as Elizabeth stood, silent and seething with barely-repressed rage at the double treachery of her sister and Lucia. It was time to make her peace with her husband. She needed all her allies at this time. Revenge would be sweet. She softly repeated the half-remembered words of King Lear to herself. "I will have such revenges on you both that all the world shall—I will do such things— what they are yet I know not, but they shall be the terrors of the earth."

ABOUT THE AUTHOR

Hugh Ashton was born in the United Kingdom, and moved to Japan in 1988, where he lived until his return to the UK in 2016.

He is best known for his Sherlock Holmes stories, which have been hailed as some of the most authentic pastiches on the market, and have received favourable reviews from Sherlockians and non-Sherlockians alike.

He has also published other work in a number of genres, including alternative history, historical science fiction, and thrillers, based in Japan, the USA and the UK

He currently lives in the historic city of Lichfield with his wife, Yoshiko.

His ramblings may be found on Facebook, Twitter, and in various other places on the Internet. He may be contacted at: author@HughAshtonBooks.com

IF YOU ENJOYED THIS STORY...

Please consider writing a review on a Web site such as Amazon or Goodreads.

You may also enjoy some adventures of Sherlock Holmes by Hugh Ashton, who has been described in *The District Messenger*, the newsletter of the Sherlock Holmes Society of London, as being "one of the best writers of new Sherlock Holmes stories, in both plotting and style".

Volumes published so far include :

Tales from the Deed Box of John H. Watson M.D.

More from the Deed Box of John H. Watson M.D.

Secrets from the Deed Box of John H. Watson M.D.

The Darlington Substitution (novel)

Notes from the Dispatch-Box of John H. Watson M.D.

Further Notes from the Dispatch-box of John H. Watson M.D.

The Death of Cardinal Tosca (novel)

The Last Notes from the Dispatch-box of John H. Watson, M.D.

The Trepoff Murder (ebook only)

1894

Without my Boswell

Some Singular Cases of Mr. Sherlock Holmes

The Lichfield Murder

The Adventure of the Bloody Steps

The Adventure of Vanaprastha (ebook only)

Children's detective stories, with beautiful illustrations by Andy Boerger, the first of which was nominated for the prestigious Caldecott Prize :

Sherlock Ferret and the Missing Necklace
Sherlock Ferret and The Multiplying Masterpieces
Sherlock Ferret and The Poisoned Pond
Sherlock Ferret and the Phantom Photographer
The Adventures of Sherlock Ferret

Short stories, thrillers, alternative history, and historical science fiction titles:

Tales of Old Japanese
At the Sharpe End
Balance of Powers
Beneath Gray Skies
Red Wheels Turning
Angels Unawares
The Untime
The Untime Revisited
Unknown Quantities

Full details of all of these and more at : https://HughAshtonBooks.com